1-2-3, I Love Thee
By: Hallie M. Williams

Illustrated by: Biswa Pathak
And Hallie M. Williams

Dedication ...

This book is dedicated to my mom and dad for sticking together and making it work. I didn't have the chance to tell them how much I loved them both, but I knew how much they cared for me.

1-2-3 is how much they loved me!

Dottie the bear
was sitting one day

and asked Grover Bear in a
very nice way

"Grover Bear, how much do you love me?"

"Easy, Dottie Bear," Grover replied with glee.

LIKE ONE-TWO-THREE

Then Grover bear said,

Then Grover Bear said:

As she rubbed his belly

Then Grover bear said,

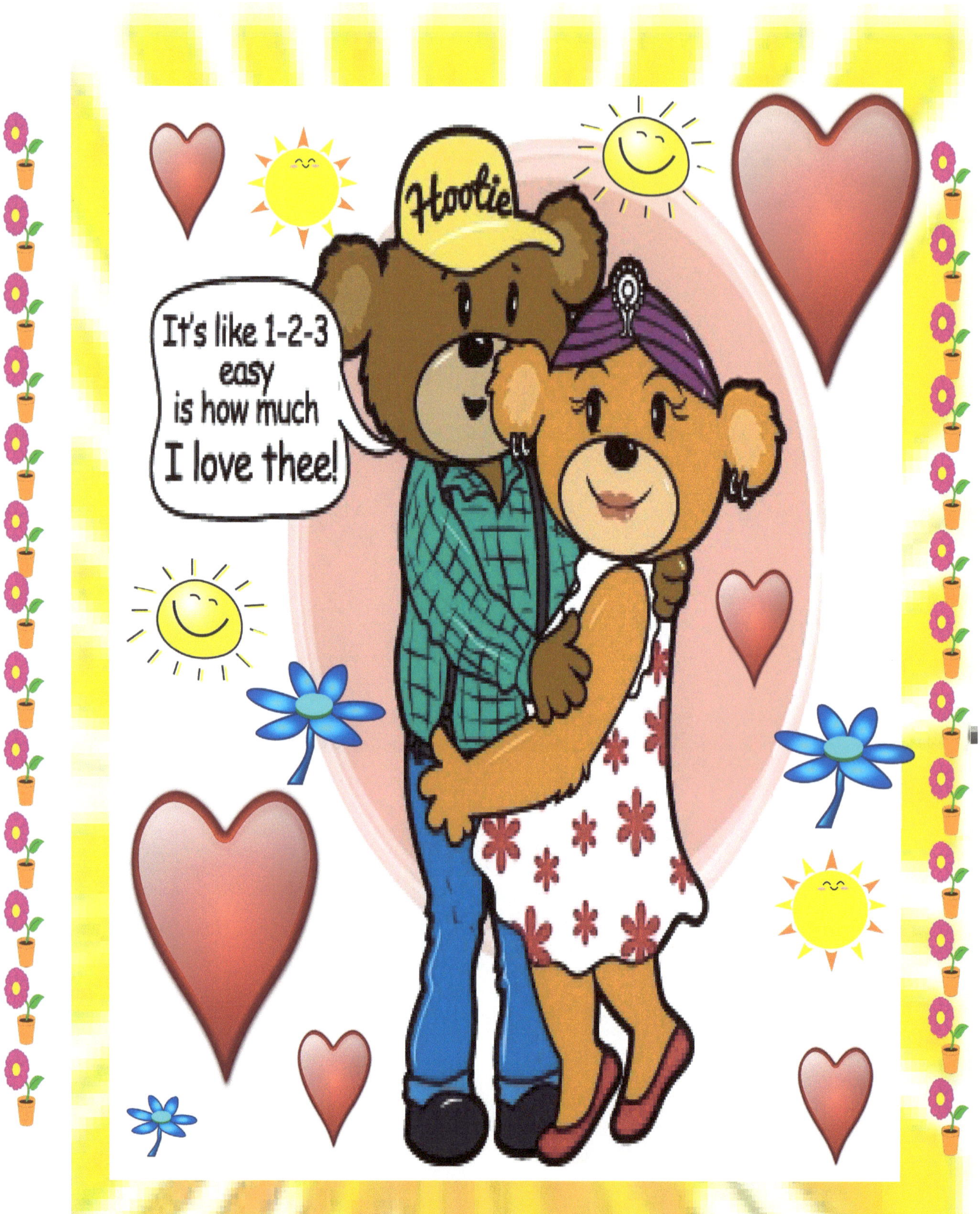
Hootie
It's like 1-2-3
easy
is how much
I love thee!

The End

About the Author...

Hallie M. Williams is originally from Columbus, Mississippi. She has a wonderful and loving family which was the foundation of her book.

She is the daughter of (the late) Grover and Doris Williams, whom were married for over 36 years.

They loved each other immensely and it was apparent by a young Hallie.

They were a loving couple that raised 14 children and maintained a happy home.
The book reflects many memories of their marriage.
It also encases every reflection of her parents.

Each detail embodies her mother and father.
From the hat on Grover the Bears head to Dottie Bear's shoes, are all part of their remembrance.

Hallie shared each memory of her mother and father and by ensuring each detail was captured...the hat, displays her father's nickname and the broach reflects her mother's fashionable style.

She hopes everyone enjoys the first book in the series of "HallieWood Book Productions- (I) Believe For It."

And hopes her mother and father would be proud. Enjoy...1-2-3, I LOVE THEE

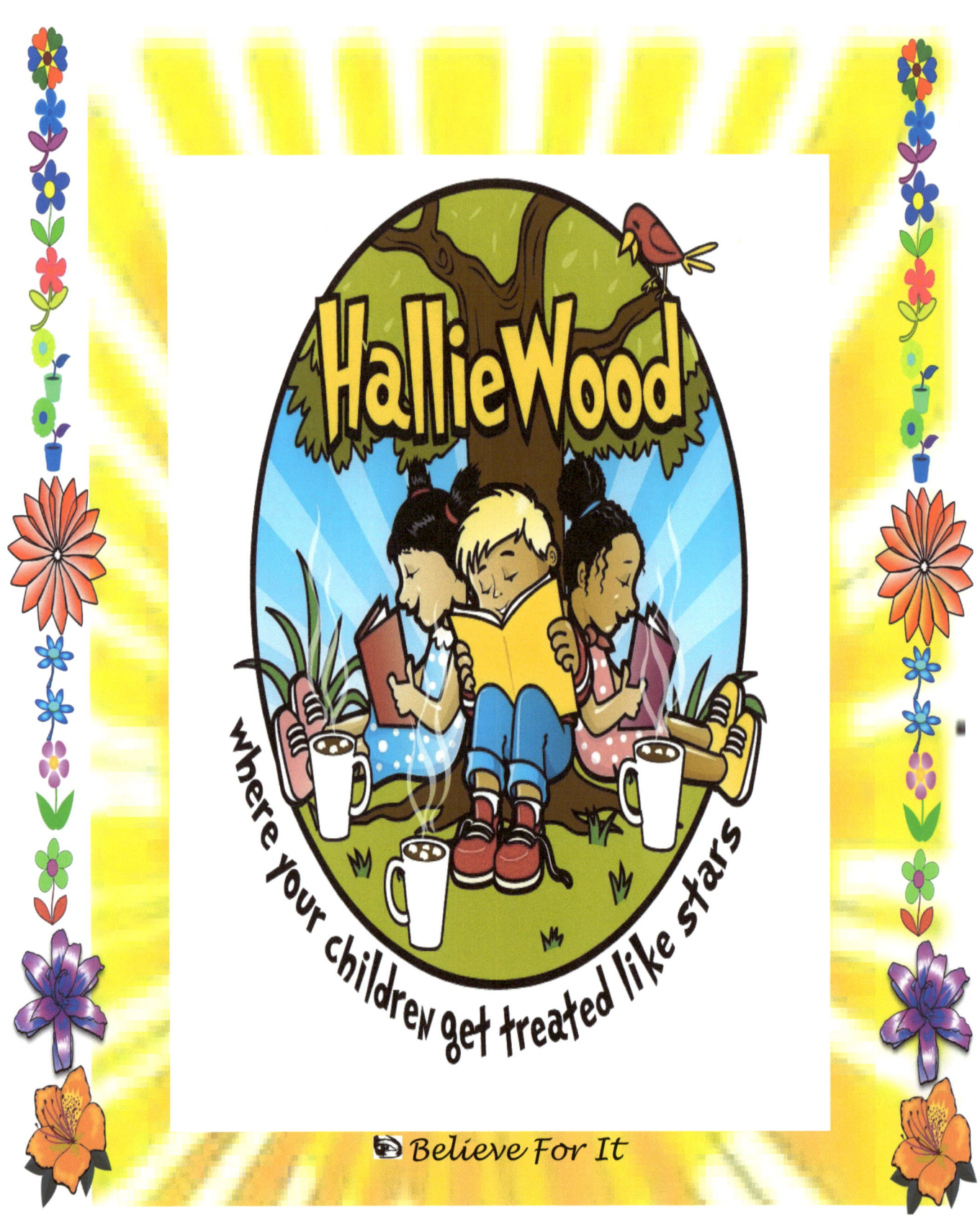

HallieWood

where your children get treated like stars

Believe For It

www.ingramcontent.com/pod-product-compliance
Lightning Source LLC
Chambersburg PA
CBHW041612120626
46551CB00002B/416